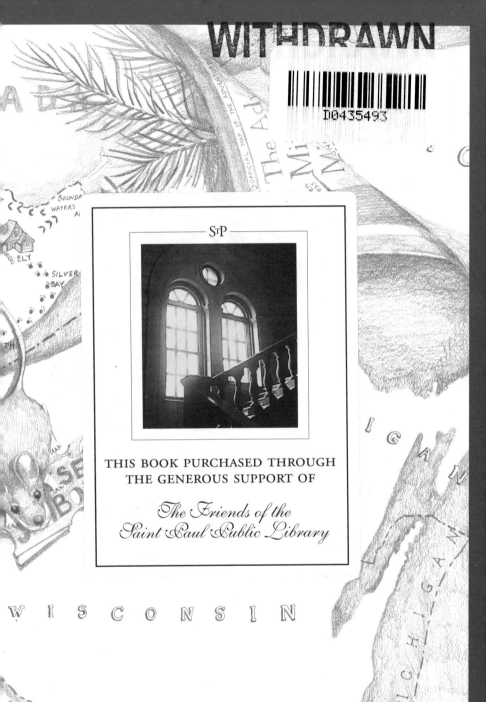

WITHDRAWN

D0435493

StP

THIS BOOK PURCHASED THROUGH
THE GENEROUS SUPPORT OF

*The Friends of the
Saint Paul Public Library*

Minn from Minnesota

by
Kathy-jo Wargin

illustrated by
Karen Busch Holman

mitten press

All inquiries should be addressed to:
Mitten Press
An imprint of Ann Arbor Media Group LLC
2500 S. State Street
Ann Arbor, MI 48104

Printed and bound by Edwards Brothers, Ann Arbor, Michigan, USA.

10   9   8   7   6   5   4   3   2   1

Library of Congress Cataloging-in-Publication Data

Wargin, Kathy-jo.
Minn from Minnesota / by Kathy-jo Wargin ; illustrated by Karen
Busch Holman.
p. cm.
Summary: When a white-footed mouse is snatched from the
northwoods cabin she shares with an elderly animal rescuer, she
endures many dangerous adventures and narrow escapes throughout the state of Minnesota as she tries to find her way back home.
ISBN-13: 978-1-58726-304-0 (hardcover : alk. paper)
ISBN-10: 1-58726-304-1 (hardcover : alk. paper)
[1. White-footed mouse--Fiction. 2. Mice--Fiction. 3. Animals --Fiction.
4. Minnesota--Fiction.]   I. Holman, Karen Busch,
1960-   , ill. II. Title.
PZ7.W234Min 2006
[E]--dc22
2006016253

Book design by Somberg Design
www.sombergdesign.com

Contents

CHAPTER ONE
The Cabin

There was nothing Minn loved more than waking to the sound of Gerdie humming in the cabin. Minn lived in the top drawer of her bureau, between scraps of old flannel blankets, tattered wool scarves, and warm knit hats that Gerdie no longer wore. The chest of drawers was painted blue with yellow flowers around its knobs, and Gerdie said it looked lovely years ago. Even though it was now scuffed and faded, the top drawer was always warm and smelled of cedar, and Minn liked it very much.

Gerdie had lived in the north woods all her life. Her parents had come to Minnesota from Sweden, so Gerdie spoke Swedish words every now and then. She took care of hurt or orphan animals from the area and was well known for doing so. She made the best homemade cheese anyone had ever tasted and baked the darkest brown bread anyone had ever seen. It seemed as if everybody knew Gerdie and liked her very much, and Minn was proud to live with her in the cabin.

Minn did not remember much about coming to Gerdie's cabin to live, but Gerdie reminded Minn of the story every morning as she ate crisp Swedish crackers called hardtack and tasty cheese for breakfast.

"Minn," Gerdie always began, "when I found you in the bushel of cherries you were a sight to behold! Never before had I seen such a small baby mouse trying to hide in my cherries." With that, Gerdie always laughed in the soft gentle way that older ladies will laugh, and broke the hard

tack crackers into pieces so that Minn
could taste some too.

The cherries had been delivered to
Gerdie's home in the woods, not far from
the town of Ely. Gerdie loved to bake with
cherries from Michigan, so every summer
the cousin of an old friend would bring her
a bushel. From this Gerdie made sweet
pies and cherry tarts, cherry jam, and cider.
But most of all, Gerdie made a special
cherry cheese that was more delicious
than any cheese Minn had ever tasted. The
two of them would sit for hours nibbling

pieces, and Minn would say, in the spirited way that a young mouse will say, that someday she was going to run away to the world's biggest cheese-eating contest. They would both laugh, and then Gerdie would say in return, "If anyone could win a cheese-eating contest, it would be you, Minn."

Even though Minn told Gerdie many times that she was going to run away and win a cheese-eating contest, she knew deep inside that she would never do such a thing. The log cabin was a nice place to live, and Minn liked how there were many things to keep her busy. Each day the plank floor needed sweeping, the fireplace needed tending, quilts needed airing, and the rounds of cheese in the drying room needed turning. Minn would sit on Gerdie's shoulder through each task, admiring everything about her from the way her gray-white hair made soft curls around her face, to the plaid wool shirt-jacket she wore with two front pockets always filled with sunflower seeds. Most of all, Minn liked the golden locket Gerdie wore around her neck. It was small and heart-shaped, and Gerdie said it was her most favorite thing of all because it was a gift from her son long ago. One day, when Minn asked where her son lived, Gerdie's expression changed. Her face went sad and she wiped the corner of her eye with the back of her hand. Then she spoke in a voice so quiet Minn barely heard her. "He's far away, very far away." Minn always remembered that day as the only time she saw Gerdie cry.

Gerdie was a good mother to Minn, and Minn knew she was lucky to have such a watchful keeper. Because of this, the little mouse never longed for anyone else, nor wondered if she had family in any other places. As it is with many white-footed mice, Minn was happy to live in a warm home with good food and a safe place to sleep. And every night when Gerdie gently placed Minn into the top drawer for safe-keeping, she would stroke the little mouse on the top of the head and softly say, *"Enda barn, kart barn,"* which was Swedish for "only child, dear child."

CHAPTER TWO

Paavo's Housewarming

Minn and Gerdie finished chores quickly so they could prepare for Paavo's housewarming. Paavo was an orphan red fox that lived in a tangle of black spruce and white cedar trees, not far from Gerdie's cabin. One day when Paavo was a young kit, her mother and father did not come back to their den as they had promised. Paavo waited there for many days, growing

thin. When Gerdie learned of this, she hungry and adopted the fox kit to make certain she was protected and well fed. The little red fox was small and wary, and Gerdie fed her meals of hamburger and oatmeal, cooked eggs and berries. When Paavo grew stronger, Gerdie hid the food in places a fox should learn to search, teaching Paavo skills she would need in nature. When Paavo was grown and Gerdie was certain she could make it on her own, she brought her to the black spruce trees where she was found and left her there to live the way a red fox should live in nature. Paavo had been there for nearly two months now, and word just came that she was doing well. She had discovered an empty rabbit den to use as her own and had sent an invitation for Gerdie, Minn, and the others to come see it.

"Minn," said Gerdie, "we need to bring wool scraps and a pail filled with red raspberries. The scraps will warm the den, and Paavo can eat the red raspberries for a treat." Minn thought that sounded like a nice housewarming present for Paavo. To let Gerdie know she agreed, Mitt nuzzled into her shoulder as they began their walk through the woods to Paavo's new den. It was early October and the birch and maple trees were splashes of bright color in the evergreen forest. Minn thought it was a beautiful day to see her old friend.

Upon their arrival they found the den hidden between the roots of a large, upturned spruce tree. Paavo was standing on top of it, greeting everyone as they arrived. She was especially excited to see Gerdie and Minn, and gave them light touches with her nose. There was loud chattering in the branches above, and Minn instantly knew it was Ratatosk. Ratatosk was an eastern gray squirrel known for his constant bickering and insults. He was whistling and

chirping at Minn and Gerdie as well as the other animals joining them. While the others seemed bothered by the fuss, Minn was only amused. She jumped off Gerdie's shoulder and climbed up the tree to sit at the old fellow's side. With an impish grin and paw on his tail she said, "Hey squirrel, I'm nuts about you!" The others waiting below began to laugh, sending Ratatosk into his hole for good. Caught up in the merriment, Minn announced to the others, "And our friend Floris wants to tell you all to eat, stink, and be merry!" Floris, an eastern striped skunk with a good sense of humor, stuck her tail straight up in the air, joining Minn in the banter.

Gerdie laughed too and placed the scraps of wool inside Paavo's den. She set the pail of raspberries outside, not far from the entrance.

"Minn," said Gerdie, "I have to go home now. You may stay

for a while, but please come home before dark."

"All by myself?" asked Minn in the wary way a mouse who is not used to being on her own will ask.

Gerdie answered, "I'm sure you'll be fine, it's not very far. Remember Minn, worry gives a small thing a big shadow." Minn thought about it and agreed, and went back to join the party.

But little did she know what would happen next.

CHAPTER THREE

Rink

When Gerdie
was out of sight,
Rink came rustling in
through the trees. He was wild with anger
and began kicking at the top of the den
with his long legs, hoping to disturb the
guests inside. Rink, a very large common
raven, was mad he hadn't been invited to
the party. His jet-black wings knocking
back and forth in the air, he was shaking

his head and making a low throaty Bronk! Bronk! Bronk! This was Rink's way of saying, in the way that ravens will do, that he had come to the party with one idea in mind—to ruin it.

The animals huddled inside. Sulo the common raccoon pulled his tail over his face. Finn the wood duck plopped down on his belly while Minn nestled into Paavo's soft white undersides. Aapo the pine marten cowered with two arctic shrews and a woodland jumping mouse. Gus the moose calf had just arrived with a mouthful of autumn willows for Paavo and did not like the threat that Rink was making. The young moose stuck his nose inside the den, trying to hide from the bird. Being so young he thought if he could not see Rink, then perhaps Rink could not see him.

But this did only one thing. It made Rink madder.

Rink began to tear away at the sticks that covered the top of Paavo's den, and Minn grew furious. How dare he ruin Paavo's new home, she thought. Minn knew Rink very well, and the two had never been friends. Rink had lived with Gerdie last year when he was brought to her with a broken jaw. During that time he often had tantrums and tore the cabin to pieces. One time he shredded the curtains and knocked over Gerdie's best blue vase of flowers. He even ripped pages from books and spilled spices all over the kitchen. One day, Gerdie lost her patience and told him that she would be glad to see him get better and fly away.

Deep inside, Rink felt sad that Gerdie wasn't as fond of him as she seemed of the others, especially Paavo and Minn.

"What will we do?" Paavo the fox asked the others. Minn told Gus to distract Rink for just a moment. The moose pulled his head out of the den and Rink flew right at him, just as Minn hoped. This gave Minn a moment to fill the others in on her plan.

In an instant, the animals bolted out of the den, each grabbing a raspberry from the bucket.

Minn climbed to the top of the den and called out to Rink, in the way that a very mad mouse will do, to come and get it. Rink's eyes flashed when he saw Minn and the others coming out to face him. He pushed out his wings as far as they could go and came straight for Minn. Then BAM! Minn hit him right between the eyes with a big fat raspberry, making a huge mess all over his face. Rink was not amused.

Feeling the triumph of her toss, Minn shouted out to the nasty bird, "This is no housewarming party. This is a mouse

warming party!" At that, the others threw their berries too, laughing at Rink, who was well deserving of a few red raspberries.

All of this was enough to make Rink fly away, and Minn danced upon Paavo's den as she watched him leave. The others joined her, feeling that justice had been served. But little did Minn know that Rink, a very large common raven with a nasty temper, was thinking up a plan all his own.

CHAPTER FOUR
Rink's Revenge

When the party finished and the last guest was gone, Minn told Paavo it was time for her to leave as well.

The early evening wind blew through the trees, and the forest clattered with the brittle sound that falling leaves make as they

spin to the forest floor. The evergreens rustled against each other, making a soft whooshing noise, and in the distance Minn could hear the waves from Bear Island Lake slapping upon the shore.

The little mouse ran across fallen logs and through thickets of young fir trees. She had a close call when a northern saw-whet owl tried to catch her, but it gave up quickly when it spotted a flying squirrel to chase instead.

When Minn saw the cabin, she raced through the door and right to Gerdie who was sitting at the table with a bowl of soup and a thick slice of brown bread. The cabin was filled with the smell of wood smoke and cinnamon, and Minn was happy to be home. She told Gerdie all about Paavo's den, Gus and Sulo, Rink, and the raspberries. Because she was wise in the ways of animals, Gerdie knew exactly what Minn was saying and took her warm hand and touched Minn softly between the ears, offering her a morsel of warm bread with butter. That night, after a dessert of sugar cookies and warm cream by the fire, Gerdie placed Minn in the top drawer and shut it almost closed, leaving just a small opening for Minn to use when she woke up in the morning. Gerdie crawled into her own bed knowing that Minn was settled, and that night the two of them listened to the sound of barred owls in the woods and a common loon crying on the far side of the lake. That night the last thing Minn remembered was hearing Gerdie quietly whisper, *"Enda barn, kart barn."* And then they both fell asleep.

Next thing Minn knew, it was morning, and there was a disturbing Whap, whap, whap! on the dresser. It was rapid and loud and rattled her drawer. Whap, whap, whap! Whap, whap, whap! Minn dared not move, for she had no idea what could be making such noise and trouble.

It was Rink.

CHAPTER FIVE

The Locket

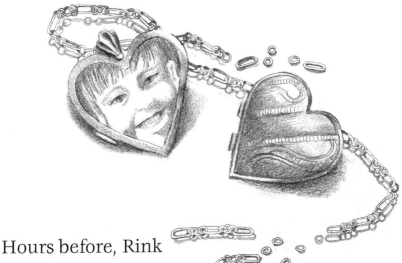

Hours before, Rink had climbed through a torn window screen to wait for Minn to wake. Rink knew that Gerdie was out on the water fishing for walleye and wouldn't be returning until noon.

Rink searched the cabin for Minn, knocking over books and turning over pictures

on the fireplace mantel. All the while, Minn stayed quiet in the drawer. The raven searched and poked and flew around, but still couldn't find her. That's when he spotted Gerdie's locket.

Gerdie had left it on the dresser so nothing would happen to it while she was fishing. Rink gave up on finding Minn and decided to break the locket instead. He was mad, and this seemed like a mad thing to do.

While Minn was still hiding in her drawer, Rink hopped on the dresser, took the heart-shaped piece in his bill, and smashed it in two. He ripped at the chain with his jaw, sending links flying this way and that. He was almost finished destroying it when he heard Gerdie returning. Quickly, he raced out the broken screen to wait in a nearby tree.

When Minn heard Rink leave, she climbed out of the drawer and onto the dresser, unaware she was standing in the middle of Gerdie's broken locket. There were tiny gold pieces all around her, and the heart was broken in two. When Gerdie walked in, she took one look at the mouse and put her hand over her heart. "Oh, Minn," she cried, "how could you?"

CHAPTER SIX
Rink's Return

Minn saw the pieces of locket all around her. She chattered away in the hasty manner that an upset mouse will do, but this time, Gerdie had no idea what Minn was trying to say. She was too upset to listen. She just picked up the pieces, held them tightly in her hands, and began to cry.

At first, Minn wanted to run away, but something deep inside told her not to. When Gerdie looked around and saw the torn curtains and fallen books, she knew that Minn could never have caused so much damage. And so she told Minn, "First things first, I must go to town to have my locket repaired. When I return, I want you to tell me who did this."

Minn let Gerdie know, in the way that a frightened mouse will do, that she would be glad to let her know who broke the locket. But what Minn didn't know was that just outside the window, Rink was listening to every word. Now he had no choice but to get Minn and take her far away for good, before she had a chance to tell Gerdie the truth.

The moment Gerdie left, Rink came bolting through the torn window screen, grabbed Minn in his bill, and shot straight

out again. He began to fly west, lofting up and above the forest, gliding smoothly over the Boundary Waters Canoe Area Wilderness.

Minn struggled against his hold, scared because she had no idea where he was taking her or what his plans were. She hollered and chirped, hoping Gerdie would hear her cry for help. She was wedged tight between his upper and lower jaw. Minn remembered that because of the injury that brought him to Gerdie in the first place, Rink could not eat properly. This, decided Minn, was probably a good thing.

The midafternoon air current pushed in from the east, moving Rink westward along a dense swampland near Upper Red Lake. Rink flew all through the night, making good time on the waves of the wind. At the first break of morning light, Rink came to a large dense marshland, edged with cattails and willows. From Minn's view there were ponds, and fields, and forests everywhere, and she had no idea where they were. And right then, in the middle of nowhere, Rink let go, dropping Minn into the dark, ice-cold water. And then he left.

CHAPTER SEVEN

Runa

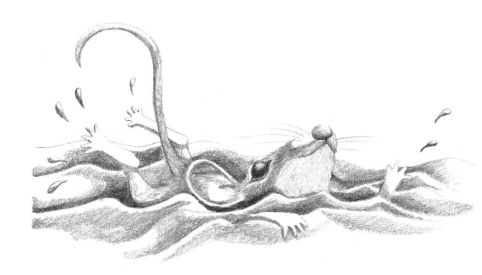

Splash! Minn fell like a tiny ball from the sky. The pond water at Agassiz National Wildlife Refuge was burning cold, and Minn was not a good swimmer. But even so, she began to paddle for the reedy shore not far from her sight. As she did, her movement made small ripples and splashes, attracting all sorts of attention at the marsh. But it wasn't the right sort of attention. Within moments, a hungry northern pike was swimming below her, waiting for the right chance to bite, while a red-tailed hawk circled above.

Minn struggled. Her paws fought the water, and she was so cold every breath seemed to get caught in her throat. She was making very little progress when, all of a sudden, whoosh! She was caught in the grasp of a long, black bill and soaring above the pond. The trumpeter swan was Runa, and she had spotted the mouse tumbling into the water. It was a good thing, too, for she had rescued Minn just in time.

Runa brought Minn to shore and released her in a thick wedge of reeds and willows. The air was harsh and bitter, and Minn was nearly frozen to death from her dip in the pond. Her coat was covered in thin layers of ice and her ears could barely move.

Runa did not have children of her own but had always wanted them and was eager to care for the mouse. The intention in the swan's heart was as beautiful as her form, which was white and billowing like a full summer cloud. Her neck was long and softly bent, and her bill was thick and black. Her dark eyes glistened upon her white face like tiny black beads set upon a drift of snow. Best of all, her feathers were dense and full, and her outstretched wing told Minn to come closer, to cuddle beneath her and warm herself.

Gathering warmth from Runa, Minn spoke through her tears, telling Runa how she was far from home. She told about Gerdie and the cabin, Paavo's housewarming and Ratatosk. She told about Rink and the rasp-berries, and Gerdie's broken locket. While Minn was speaking, more swans joined them, settling around Runa and Minn to listen.

When Minn finished her story, Runa raised her head and spoke above the others. "We must take her! We must take her!"

But the other swans looked away, trying very hard to ignore Runa's request. They were afraid to go east, for the water was freezing quickly. They needed to be fur-ther south now and had no time to spare.

Runa called out again, "We must take her! We must take her!" But still the swans did not respond. One by one they slipped back onto the water and floated to the far side of the pond. Seeing them leave, Minn thought she would be left at the refuge forever, with no way to survive.

But Runa didn't leave. Even though her flock disagreed, Runa couldn't bear to see the mouse left behind. She had almost been a mother once but had lost her eggs to a great horned owl. When that happened, she made a promise that she would never let such a thing happen again, and even though it was a mouse, she was going to keep her word.

And so Runa lowered her neck to Minn's level, looked her straight in the eyes, and whispered the words Minn was hoping to hear, *"I will take you home."*

CHAPTER EIGHT
The Blizzard

Runa lifted off over Agassiz and, as she began her flight, was joined in ranks by her flock. "We will come," they sang, "we will come!" Runa was joyful for their change of heart, and Minn found comfort in their company. "I will be home in no time," thought Minn, who snuggled into Runa's upper back, grasping the downy underside of her feathers. Minn watched the other swans flying alongside Runa, beating their way east, their long wings falling into a rhythm of soundless flight across the north country.

As they made their way, the wind gathered strength. It began blowing harder bit by bit, working against them as they flew east along Red Lake River. Because of this, they chose to take a southern route below Lower Red Lake rather than crossing over it where the wind would be even stronger.

As they flew, however, the sky rolled into darkening shades of winter gray, which only deepened by the hour. The wind

fought their wings and stung their eyes, and their senses told them something was changing. And then it began to snow.

It was not a gentle snow, but a driving snow that came upon them fast. Minn closed her eyes while the wind moaned over the tops of the birds, fighting to keep their southeast course. It was certain now, the swans had no choice but to descend.

One by one, they landed in a forest not far from Itasca State Park, seven white swans upon the snow, folding their heads into their wings and bedding down for shelter.

The storm raged while they huddled to stay warm. Some of them made low distressing calls, while others just kept quiet. Runa knew, as the others did, this was going to be a blizzard.

The swans remained nestled together for hours while the storm continued. Hour by hour, Minn grew colder, and so she made a tunnel to burrow herself deep in a pocket of snow far beneath Runa, who was unaware that Minn was doing such a thing. It was there, beneath layers of snow that worked as a blanket to keep Minn warm, that the tired mouse fell asleep.

The swans remained as long as they could, but the moment the storm lessened, they understood their hunger and knew, in the way that swans know, it was time to seek open water for food. This was how it was when winter came early to the north, and the swans knew what to do. But it also meant they would not be able to bring Minn home now, but rather, they would have to bring her south with them and return her to Ely in the spring.

In the middle of the night, the swans took flight. Thinking Minn was safe and sound and fast asleep in the underside of her top feathers, Runa joined them.

The next morning, Minn poked her head out of the snow. "Runa," Minn cried. "Runa, where are you? Runa come back, I'm right here!" Minn's shrill cries filled the forest, but it was too late. The swans were gone.

CHAPTER NINE

The Woodsman

Minn looked around the woods and, though she was frightened, found beauty in the way they were quiet and heavy with snow after the storm.

Minn didn't know whether to be grateful that Runa had taken her this far, or sad because she had been left behind. Either way, she realized that what she felt most deeply now was hunger, so she raced

across the snow in search of food, crossing fallen trees and running between large stands of Norway and white pines. She had a hard time finding food and nibbled on pieces of bark that had come loose from trees during the storm.

The forest was made of long rolling hills and small kettle-shaped lakes, most not yet frozen but only days away from being so.

Minn reached a red pine that had been snapped in an earlier storm and spotted a

hole in which to make her way to the inside. She was happy to do so, as it would provide shelter and warmth. But as she was doing so, a large shadow fell over her. And it wasn't an eagle. It was bigger. Much bigger.

Minn turned to see a large man standing over her. He was as tall as five men, and his shoulders were as broad as a house. He had a thick dark beard and hearty laugh, and took Minn in his hand.

"And where do you think you're going?" his voice boomed. "How about you come along with me, lil' friend. I'll get you warmed up and make you soup."

Minn shuddered. She did not know why such a large woodsman would want to take a mouse. And she didn't like the sound of being warmed up or made into soup, if that's what he meant. He did say "make you soup," which could mean he would either make her some soup, or make her into soup.

Either way, the woodsman was much bigger than any man she had ever seen, and so Minn thought she better not make a fuss about being taken. The woodsman walked to a clearing in the woods where he had set up camp and placed Minn on a log. He pulled out a large pot and said, "Better a mouse in the pot than no meat at all!"

Minn gulped, in the way a frightened mouse will do. But before her fear was allowed to grow, the woodsman quickly laughed and said, "I'm just a kiddin'. That's just a little somethin' my momma used to say, way back when in the old days."

Minn was relieved when the woodsman put the kettle on the fire and began to tell stories. He told how he was such a big baby that his mother had to put his cradle out to sea, and how when he was a young man he found a big blue ox in the snow. He told Minn how he made all the lakes just by taking a walk, and that sometimes when he's hungry, it takes five men to grease the griddle. Minn listened, warming herself by the fire and feasting on bread crumbs and broth. Once comfortable, she told the woodsman about Gerdie and the cabin, and how Runa left her behind.

The woodsman enjoyed Minn's company but even so, felt he should bring her home. "By the end of the day, my friend," said the woodsman, "you will be home for good. I will bring you there in ten big steps. But first," he went on to say, "I need to cut down a few more trees and bundle them together. Then we can go."

Minn was overjoyed knowing she would be home before bedtime. Tonight she would

cuddle with Gerdie and hear the words
Enda barn, kart barn before she fell asleep.
Minn hung onto the woodsman's broad
shoulder as they went deeper into the forest. The head of his axe was as big as a
barn door, and when the woodsman took a
swing, it went wide and straight. Minn was
trying to hang on as best she could, but
when the blade hit the tree, the force was
more than she could take. The woodsman
hollered, "Timber!" and Minn went flying
off his shoulder and through the air. He
hollered so loud it rang through seven
counties, and nobody could hear Minn's
cries for help.

Except the owl.

The great horned owl was Trigg, and his
tufted ears poked out from his head like
feathered spikes, while his straw-colored
eyes caught the sunshine as it fell upon
his gray-brown face. He was perched in a

nearby red pine tree, and although Trigg rarely flew during the day, he had been awoken by the disturbance. Now alert, he decided to go on a hunt.

When he heard the woodsman holler "timber" and saw the little mouse fly from his shoulder, he knew it wouldn't take much to snatch it. And he did. Before Minn knew what happened, Trigg was flying into the woods with a mouse clamped in his feet and one thing on his mind. To eat her.

CHAPTER TEN

The Swensons

The Swenson family had been snowshoe-
ing since early morning, eager to explore
the freshly fallen snow. The father broke
trail while the mother followed, carrying
a small knapsack on her back. The girl
was dressed in a bright red-and-blue
parka, with a hat to match. Her name was

Anna Lena, and, although not more than eight years old, she kept pace with her mother, her wooden snowshoes making a soft whoomfing sound upon the snow.

The family was walking over a big hill when a snowshoe hare crossed in front of them. It was running very fast, and Anna Lena squealed with delight. Behind it was a great horned owl with a mouse in its grasp. The family watched as the owl flew inches above their heads. Caught in the hurry of his chase, Trigg dropped the mouse in order to gain speed. The family watched the owl closing on the hare, both going deeper into the forest and out of sight. At their feet lay a small, white-footed mouse, and she was nearly dead.

Minn was stunned and barely able to move. The father reached down and placed her in his gloved hand. "There, there, little one, it's okay now." Anna Lena and her mother gathered round and quickly knew what to do.

"We must warm it up," said Anna Lena, "and feed it."

The father smiled and the mother opened the knapsack. She took a handful of cereal and some corners of cheese. Anna Lena found a spare wool scarf and placed Minn comfortably inside. They spoke softly and gently to Minn, and there in the woods of Paul Bunyan State Forest, she was saved.

At least for now.

CHAPTER ELEVEN
Maple Ridge Farm

It took a couple of hours to get to their home near Alexandria. It was called Maple Ridge Farm, and it was one of the tidiest farms Minn could imagine. There was a freshly painted white fence all around, and a bright yellow house with fancy white trim. There were three barns, two small red ones with yellow trim and one large

white one with four windows and a weather vane, and a chicken coop. There were Jersey cows outside one of the small red barns and several horses in a corral not far beyond.

Anna Lena brought Minn into the big white barn to introduce her to the animals. There was a brown Swiss dairy cow in one stall and a large American cream draft horse in the other. Each stall had a window and a bucket. Piles of winter hay were set neatly in one corner, and there was a red painted bench with a flowered cushion beneath the largest window nearest the barn doors. Anna Lena carefully showed Minn to the cow.

"This is Britta," she said to Minn. "Britta stays inside most of the time and will be good company for you." Minn thought Britta was the color of an autumn wheat field, her coat all shades of dusky brown

and tan. Britta looked at Minn in the careful way an unsure cow will do and then went back to eating her hay. The horse was another matter. His name was Finn. Although he was as handsome and hearty as Minn had ever seen, he was a bit on the cranky side, flaring his nostrils and bucking his head up and down as Anna Lena brought the mouse closer. "Don't worry too much about him," said the girl, "he's much nicer than he looks."

With that, Anna Lena made Minn a bed out of an old cheese crate, filling it with hay and an old horse blanket. She placed the crate high on a tack shelf where Minn would be safe. Minn was happy to have a warm place to sleep, but kept thinking about how to get home. When Anna Lena turned out the barn light and said good-night, the moonlight filled each of the four square windows, casting uneven blue shadows throughout the barn. Minn watched Britta and Finn sleep and wondered if Gerdie was snuggled in bed too, beneath the same moon, wondering where she was. *"Enda barn, kart barn,"* Minn said to herself. Only child, dear child.

Minn was alone.

CHAPTER TWELVE

Blix

Minn woke to the moan of heavy wooden doors opening, the tin ring of metal pails being carried to and fro, and the gentle earthy scrape of hay being tossed into the barn for morning feeding. Anna Lena burst into the barn to check on Minn and was happy to see that the mouse looked much better than when it arrived. Anna Lena carefully fed Minn oats and sunflower seeds by hand while stroking her gently on the top of her head. Minn liked it when she did so, as it reminded her of being home with Gerdie.

Anna Lena had many chores to do for such a young girl. When Minn finished telling Anna Lena all about Gerdie and how much she wanted to go home, Anna Lena got an idea.

"If you help me with chores all winter, at the first sign of spring I will see to it that you get home."

Minn thought this sounded like a fair bargain. From that day on, when Anna Lena swept the barn, Minn was right there with her, using her tail to sweep up spilled oats and her nose to push pieces of straw back into the stalls. When Anna Lena needed to brush Finn, Minn would hop up and

smooth out his mane, to make it look handsome and well groomed. And when Anna
Lena needed to collect eggs from the chick-
ens in the other barn, Minn would go along
too, following close behind to make sure
no eggs were forgotten.

But all the time, Minn was watching for spring. She would feel the air with her whiskers to see if it had warmed and watch the earth for the first new flowers to poke through the snow.

Being busy was a good thing for a mouse such as Minn, for the winter did pass quickly this way. One day, as Minn was following Anna Lena to the chicken coop, she saw a tiny crocus poking its way out of the snow.

"Anna Lena," shouted Minn, "it's time to bring me home, it's spring!"

Anna Lena looked down at the crocus and shook her head no, as if to say the bargain was off.

"But you promised!" said Minn. "You promised to bring me home at the first sign of spring!"

Anna Lena began to walk away, and this made Minn very mad.

"Wait just one minute," chirped Minn, in the way a mouse will do when it has been wronged. "I worked all winter for you because you promised to see that I get home. A promise is a promise!"

Anna Lena lowered her eyes as her chin began to quiver.

"But I can't drive," said Anna Lena. "How would I get you anywhere? I'm too little."

"Can you walk there? Can you ride a bike?" asked Minn, gaining hope.

"No, no silly, it's much too far," responded Anna Lena.

"Well then," said Minn, thinking clearly, "can Britta or Finn take me home?"

"It's much too far for them too. Britta is old and Finn is slow."

The pair sat outside the chicken coop for quite some time. The rooster was crowing, the sheep were making all sorts of noise, and the young horses in the far field were racing back and forth.

"Wait!" said Anna Lena. "I have an idea. I'll be right back."

When Anna Lena returned, she was holding a young red colt by the reins. The colt was Blix, and he was tall and thin and fast. He had a wild look in his eyes that told Minn he wasn't quite ready for riders yet, and Minn scrambled backward.

"Here's my idea," said Anna Lena, leaning down to speak to Minn. "Blix will take you."

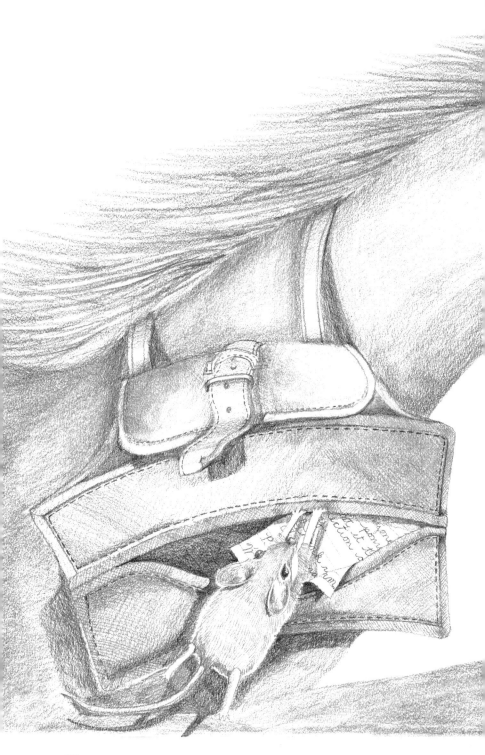

Blix was young, yet even so had ripples of muscle all through his flanks and a black mane that was full and well groomed.

He belonged to Anna Lena, but Anna Lena herself had not yet ridden him. The horse stared at the mouse. He lifted one foot upward and placed it down heavily, then lifted the other and did the same. All the while, he was blowing air through his nostrils, making a loud whooshing sound each time.

Minn hesitated. "Does he like mice?" Minn asked nervously.

Anna Lena pretended not to hear the question, because in truth, she wasn't very sure if the pony liked mice at all. But to her, it was a very small detail.

Anna Lena grabbed Minn and placed her in a green canvas sack. She hung the sack around Blix's neck and added a note that read, "If anyone finds this pony, please point it in the direction of Ely. Thank you. Anna Lena. PS: The pony belongs to Maple Ridge Farm."

It was dark and damp and smelly inside the rucksack, but at least it was a start, and

Minn was eager to get home. Anna Lena whispered something into the colt's ear and gave it a firm pat on the rear. The pony reared up and raced out of Maple Ridge and Anna Lena cheered. Minn bumped up and down in the sack, trying to settle in for the ride. As she worked to hang on, she remembered something Gerdie always told her—"It's too late to shut the stable door after the horse has bolted." The ride was getting rougher and bumpier by the minute, and Minn finally understood what Gerdie meant when she said those words.

But Minn didn't know that Blix was not her biggest problem. It was the rucksack. There was a hole in the bottom, and Minn was bouncing all the way through it.

CHAPTER THIRTEEN

The *Tomten*

Minn spilled out onto the road. She rolled
and she bounced, she went spinning and
turning. She landed in a ditch half filled
with melting snow. As she got her bear-
ings, she took one look around and noticed
one thing. Blix was long gone.

Minn crawled out of the ditch and into the
first patch of forest edge she could find. As

she sat there gaining her wits, she heard a voice cry out, "Help, help me! Help me!" Minn couldn't tell where the sound was coming from and so went to find it. She scrambled deeper into the woods, which was mostly young shrubs and saplings and thickets with thorns and thistles. When she reached the middle, what she saw there took her by surprise.

It was a very small person, not much larger than a squirrel, carrying an egg.

"I need help with this egg! I need help or it will break," the tiny boy shouted. The egg was almost as large as he was, and it was creamy white with brown speckles. Minn rushed to his side and helped roll the egg with her nose as the little boy pushed it with his hands. They rolled it along until they came to a mound of old grass. "That's the nest I made to help it hatch," said the boy proudly. "What do you think?"

Minn didn't think it was much of a nest, and so asked, "Why would a boy want to hatch an egg?"

"First of all," he said, "I'm not a boy. I'm Per, and I'm a *tomten*."

"A *tomten*?" quizzed Minn. "I've never seen a *tomten* before. Are you related to a red squirrel?"

The *tomten* did not know whether to laugh or be insulted, so he decided to use a joke instead. "I'm not a squirrel, are you nuts?" the *tomten* quipped. This made Minn laugh loudly, and she knew right away she could be friends with a *tomten*.

Per went on. "I'm a helper. Every day I sneak into homes or barns and do good things for people. I clean the stalls, do the dishes, or help make gardens grow better. The people leave me porridge or other

treats to thank me. Then I leave before they see me. I come back here in the woods and hide."

"I see," said Minn. "But what about the egg?"

"I found this egg all by itself, with no mother or father to take care of it. So I made a nest out of winter grass and started to bring the egg here, but it was too heavy. So I called for help. That's when I met you!"

Minn didn't think a *tomten* would be very good at warming an egg. For the first time since Rink had dropped her into the pond over Agassiz, Minn wasn't thinking about Gerdie, or Paavo, or the warm cabin.

"I will sit on the egg for you," Minn said matter-of-factly. "I'm fatter and warmer, and I have more experience living in nests."

Minn and Per pushed the nest into a thicket of hazelnut, making sure it was out of sight. Per left, and when he came back, he had with him a tiny sack filled with seeds and oats for Minn. Minn ate well, and then the pair snuggled into the nest and shared a good night's sleep.

By morning Minn was thinking about home again. So she thought to ask, "Per, since you do good things, can you help me get home?"

"That depends," he said. "Where do you live?"

"I live up north in Ely," she said. Minn went on to tell about Gerdie and Paavo and the beautiful cabin by the lake. Per was a good listener. When Minn finished he said, "If you keep this egg warm until it hatches, I will see that you get home."

It was early spring now and the forest was still rather quiet. Minn stood a very good chance of keeping the egg safe until it hatched, so it seemed like a good idea.

Minn and Per thought the nest was well hidden and that because it was such a small stretch of forest, there would be no foxes or coyotes to worry about. But little did they know that Hod was out there, waiting for his chance to get the egg—and the mouse.

CHAPTER FOURTEEN
Hod

Minn stayed upon the egg for weeks, and it seemed that little happened in the young woods where they were hiding. The forest was turning brighter as the sun moved a bit higher each day and the first yellow lady's slippers sprang up in the woods.

Per left each morning before sunrise and returned at high noon with oats and seeds. He left again after having lunch with Minn and returned at dusk, with raisins and pumpkin bread from Mrs. Anderson's kitchen. Minn ate very well during these days and was growing fatter doing nothing but sitting on the egg. Even so, she was content and satisfied with her work.

All the while, Hod, the bobcat, had been keeping a close eye on them all, watching Minn and Per and the egg. One morning after Per left for the day, Hod decided it was time to move.

He stalked in, lifting his paws high enough so they made no noise on the forest floor. When Hod was about five steps from the thicket where Minn was hiding with the egg, he stopped to wait. He crept forward and stopped again. Hod was very patient in his approach, and with each careful step moved closer and closer. Minn was sleeping and had no idea of his presence until he SPRANG into the thicket.

Minn squealed and the noise caught the attention of two red-tailed hawks that had been circling the area looking for a mouse. The hawks were Rinda and Rane. They were big and loud and the undersides of their wings were a brilliant white with brown speckled spots. In an instant, the hawks made a quick turn. Minn watched as they came her way and she had no idea what would happen next.

The hawks swerved in, and then down. Their first move was toward Hod the bobcat. They dove and pushed until he went screaming away into the woods. They followed to make sure he was gone. And then they came back for Minn.

CHAPTER FIFTEEN

Rinda and Rane

Rinda and Rane circled the nest and Minn stood upright, drumming her foot on a dry leaf, hoping to signal for the *tomten*'s help. It was no use. Rinda swooped in and grabbed Minn while Rane gently took the egg in her talons. Minn was squirming and fighting the red-tailed hawk's grasp, squealing chit, chit, chit as she watched the other hawk carry the egg away.

And then Rinda perched in a tree, settling Minn into a crotch of its branches. Minn thought it was the end.

"Thank you," said Rinda. "Rane and I heard about you and the *tomten* who saved our baby. We have been looking for you for weeks, and now will take the egg home."

Minn was so relieved she couldn't speak. And although she was happy that she wasn't about to be eaten, deep inside she was a bit sad that she would have to part with the egg. She knew the egg did not belong to her through nature, but it seemed like it belonged to her through love.

"But first," said Rinda, "I must repay you for your kindness."

Minn wasn't entirely sure how Rinda could help, but she began her story about how she had gotten so far away from home, and how she missed Gerdie and the cabin. She told about Runa the trumpeter swan who had left her behind, even when she promised not to. She told about the woodsman and Trigg, Anna Lena and Blix. Then she quietly said, "I just want to go home. Can you take me there?"

Rinda lowered his head into his chest and took a breath before speaking. Minn could tell the bird was torn about what he needed to say. "I am sorry that I can't take you north myself. It's very far away and I can't be gone that long. You see, I need to stay with Rane and find food for her once the baby hatches. But I can take you somewhere closer."

"Closer?" asked Minn. "How will that help me get home?"

"If you trust me, let me take you. I will explain when we get there." And so Minn, being small in body but large in heart, had no other choice but to trust the hawk.

Rinda took Minn in his bill and began to fly south. He brought Minn to a rolling prairie in the corner of southwestern Minnesota and set her down upon a cliff. Rinda gestured to the open sky and said, "Wait here and you will find your way home. Others who fly are making the journey north now, and they will come this way, I promise." Rinda thanked Minn one last time and said good-bye. When he was gone, Minn felt very small sitting on the prairie. Small and lonely indeed.

CHAPTER SIXTEEN
Esket

Minn decided to make a home for herself so she would be safe while she waited. She noticed there were already many holes in the ground and so, feeling it was her good fortune, chose one and crawled in. It was a quiet place, dark and damp with the smell of freshly plowed earth. The hole worked its way into an underground maze of tun-

nels so Minn went a bit further, until she found just the right place to fall asleep. She curled into a tiny ball and began to dream of home.

But Minn had no more than closed her eyes when she heard a yip-wheeze sound. She wasn't sure what it was, so she stood upright to listen. Pretty soon the sound was coming from many places in the ground, and it turned into a chattering of yips and growls and chirps. She began to feel the earth shake a bit, and then it happened.

Hundreds of black-tailed prairie dogs came storming past. There were old ones and young ones, fat ones and small ones, and kind ones and pushy ones. Minn flattened herself against a dirt wall, hoping none would notice a trespassing mouse.

But one did.

His name was Esket. He was a young prairie dog and was unsure about a mouse in his colony. "Hey you," he snapped, "get your mouse ears out of here!"

Minn began to run. She was almost out of the hole when Esket grabbed her by the tail. It was more than she could take. She turned around and looked Esket square in the eyes. Then she let him have it.

"I am a mouse who was stolen by a raven, and then dropped in a pond and saved by a swan. I was forgotten by the swan, picked up by a woodsman who, by the way and for your information was indeed Paul Bunyan, then grabbed by an owl, and taken home with a family. I was put on a horse and fell out of a sack and landed in a ditch where I heard someone say "Help." I then met a *tomten* and sat on an egg and was almost eaten by a bobcat, then was taken by a hawk and dropped ... right ... here. Can't a mouse just get a break around here?"

Esket sat down and began to cry. He had only wanted to be her friend.

And when he told her this, Minn did the only thing she could think to do. She laughed. She rolled around in the grass and laughed as hard as she could, and Esket joined her. The pair jumped and played, weaving and hiding in the new spring grass. "Hey Esket, let's play my favorite game," said Minn.

"What's that?" asked the prairie dog.

"Hide and squeak!"

Esket began to chase Minn, but Minn had a very good head start. She ran over the grass and behind a thick gray rock with purple flowers growing out of its cracks. She hid there, hoping Esket wouldn't find her quickly. She closed her eyes tight and stayed real still. She felt the earth tremble a bit and thought it meant that Esket was coming closer.

But he wasn't.

It was something else, and it was large and dark and its shadow fell like midnight upon her.

CHAPTER SEVENTEEN
Jumping Mouse

The bison was Trond, and it wasn't his intention to find a little mouse hiding by the rock. He was simply grazing, walking slowly along the prairie eating tender pieces of grass when he decided to rub his coat along the jagged edge of the quartzite bluff. It was there he noticed the little mouse and decided to poke her with his nose.

Minn, still thinking it could be Esket, jumped up and turned around. She hadn't opened her eyes yet when she began hollering at who she thought was her prairie dog friend. "Well, it took you long enough, you little prairie weasel!" hollered Minn. And then she opened her eyes.

Trond was amused. He snorted and bellowed and shook his gigantic head back and forth, unable to believe the amount of pluck one little mouse could have.

"Allow me to introduce myself. I'm Trond, but others call me Tatanka," the bison stated. "Were you expecting someone else?"

"Tatanka?" asked Minn. "What type of word is that?" And so he told her it was a word

from the Dakota people who have lived there for hundreds of years, and in their language it means bison. When Minn told him that she was looking for her friend Esket, Trond took the time to tell the little mouse that *tinta* means prairie and *maka* means earth. "But the most important word to know is *Ina*," he said. "It means mother."

Hearing this made Minn want to cry. She was tired and weary and not quite frightened, yet not quite brave. She told Trond her story, how she was taken by a bird and dropped in the water. She told about Runa and Anna Lena, Blix and Rinda, and how Rinda told her to wait on the prairie. Most of all she spoke about Gerdie, and how much she wanted to get home to her, but no longer knew how to do it. When she finished speaking, Trond spoke.

"Your story reminds me of a story I heard many years ago on the prairie. Perhaps I could tell it to you, and it will help you find your way home." And then he began.

"Long ago, as the legend goes, there was a little mouse, like you. This mouse was very busy and wanted to know many things. He kept hearing a rushing sound in his head and did not know what it was. He asked raccoon, who told him it was the great river. The little mouse did not know what a river was, so raccoon said, 'Do not worry, I will take you there and show you.' So the mouse followed the raccoon to the river. It was very wide and the water went by very fast. It was clear and beautiful, and the mouse thought it was wonderful. At the river, raccoon introduced the mouse to a frog. The frog was sitting on a lily pad in a quiet pool along the edge of the river, and he welcomed the mouse to the river. At this, the raccoon left."

Minn sat closer. She wanted to hear every word that Trond was saying.

"The little mouse went to the water and looked at his reflection. He looked scared. 'Aren't you afraid of the water?' the mouse asked the frog. 'No, I am not afraid. I am Keeper of the Water. Would you like to have some medicine power like me?' the frog asked. Of course the mouse wanted to overcome his fear, so he said yes. The frog told the mouse, 'Crouch as low as you can and then jump as high as you can, and you will have your medicine!' So the mouse did just that, and when he was up in the air, he saw the sacred mountains. When he came down, he landed in the water and was very wet, and very scared. Even so, he was inspired by the vision he saw. And so the frog named him Jumping Mouse."

Trond looked closer at Minn, to make certain the little mouse understood his story.

"Jumping Mouse went back to the forest, but nobody believed what had happened. He could not forget the sacred mountains and wanted to see them again. One day he went to the edge of a beautiful prairie, just like this one. He looked out over the ocean of flowers and grasses, and saw eagles flying in the sky. Jumping Mouse was afraid of the eagles, but even so, he gathered his courage and ran out into the wide-open prairie. He ran into a thicket of sage, where he met a very old mouse. The old mouse welcomed him with nuts and seeds and advised Jumping Mouse to remain there, for the eagles would never spot him in such a nice thicket. But Jumping Mouse did not want to remain in a thicket. He wanted to see the sacred mountains again, and so he thanked the old mouse and left to find them. Jumping Mouse gathered his courage one more time and ran into a bush of chokecherries. It was nice there. There was plenty of food and water. There were grasses for a nest and other good things. Jumping Mouse explored his new domain and heard heavy breathing. It was a buffalo, like me. The buffalo welcomed Jumping Mouse, and the mouse noticed that it was dying. The buffalo told Jumping Mouse that he believed that only the eye of a mouse could save him."

Minn interrupted. "What did Jumping Mouse do? Did he run away?"

Trond answered.

"You see, at first Jumping Mouse did not want to give up one of his eyes, and so he hid. But then he thought about it. He went back to the buffalo and said, 'I will not let you die, I have two eyes and you may have one.' As he spoke, one eye magically flew out of his head and the buffalo was healed. He thanked Jumping Mouse and told him he would be his brother forever. He said 'I know about your trip to the river and your quest for the sacred mountains.'

"So Jumping Mouse went on his way and met brother wolf. But the wolf had a short memory and could not remember he was a wolf. He kept forgetting. Jumping Mouse knew what would heal the wolf. He told the wolf he could have his eye, and the instant he spoke, his eye flew out of his head and healed the wolf. Now Jumping Mouse was blind and had no way to find the sacred mountains. He was very scared and curled into a ball. All of a sudden an eagle grabbed him and flew away. Magically, this made Jumping Mouse fall asleep."

"Did Jumping Mouse make it to the sacred mountains?" asked Minn.

Trond didn't answer. Instead, he simply told the rest of the story.

"You see, when Jumping Mouse woke, he could see again. It was blurry, but he knew he could see. A blurry shape came forth and asked if he wanted medicine. Jumping Mouse said yes and the shape told Jumping Mouse, 'Crouch down as low as you can, and then jump as high as you can.' Jumping Mouse did, and the wind carried him higher and higher into the sky. The voice from the blurry shape told him to trust the wind.

Jumping Mouse opened his eyes again and his vision was clear. The voice was his friend the frog who was sitting on a lily pad on the lake below. The frog called out to Jumping Mouse, 'You now have a new name, and it is eagle!'"

Minn closed her eyes when Trond finished the story. She imagined herself as an eagle, flying home on a current of wind. Minn heard thunder across the prairie and opened her eyes. Trond was gone. But Esket was sitting beside her.

CHAPTER EIGHTEEN
Runa's Return

The next morning, Minn began her journey home. Esket knew the prairie well and was happy to help her. The pair headed east, scrambling across vast fetches of prairie grass and brown-eyed Susans.

The pair came to a part of the prairie northeast of where they began, and there were rocks pushing out of the grass. Minn noticed pictures on the rocks. They looked as if they were made a long time ago, and Esket began to laugh when he saw a picture of a big soaring bird. It was a thunderbird, and it reminded Minn of Rink, the common raven who started this whole mess.

Minn spotted a picture that looked like Runa, and a drawing of a shape that made her think about Gerdie. She wondered if Gerdie thought she was gone for good. "What if Gerdie thinks I ran away?" Minn asked herself. "What if she thinks I don't love her and I wanted to live somewhere else? What if she thinks I didn't want to be her *enda barn, kart barn?*" Minn's desire to get home grew and grew to the point she thought she would burst. Minn put her face into her paws and began to sob.

Being a kind friend, Esket noticed this and crawled up to Minn's side to whisper,

"Minn, why don't you crouch as low as you can, then jump as high as you can. Maybe you will be an eagle and then you can fly home? It worked for Jumping Mouse."

Minn thought about this for a moment. "What could be wrong with trying?" she thought to herself? And so on the edge of a very tall rock in the middle of a prairie, Minn crouched as low as she could. Then, she jumped as high as she could. She flew through the air and it was nothing like Esket had ever seen before. And then she began to tumble downward.

All the way down, Minn was wondering why she had done such a silly thing. She closed her eyes as tight as they could go. She was picking up downward speed when all of a sudden something changed. She felt differently. She was going up. Softly, gently, upward into the sky. Minn was amazed at how easy flying seemed to be.

She opened her eyes to see what she looked like as an eagle.

But Minn hadn't turned into an eagle. It was Runa. Runa was back and she had saved Minn, again. And although she was still a mouse, Minn was very happy all the same.

Runa flew north along the Mississippi River flyway, and Minn watched the river twist and turn below her. There were boats of all sizes and towns along its shore. Every now and again they would stop for something to eat, and the pair would chatter away and tell stories about the winter.

They stopped to feed in a pond north of the Twin Cities, and Runa was exceptionally hungry. She stuck her long neck into the pond, grabbing mouthfuls of grit from the bottom. Minn was off in the nearby field, gathering seeds and berries of her own to eat. When she finished, she came to the pond's edge to wait for Runa.

When the pair began to make their way north again, Runa stopped often, for the journey seemed to be taking a great deal of her strength. They made it to Duluth, and went along the north shore of Lake Superior and into an area of small lakes and rivers. Runa found a large dead tree near the Lester River and roosted there, telling Minn, in the way a tired swan will do, that she would need a good night's rest before they could go any further. When Minn appeared worried about getting home, Runa told her in a quiet and tender way that they would be home tomorrow and that Ely was not far away.

Once she was reassured, Minn was so excited that she couldn't sleep that night. Her journey was over and she would be back home with Gerdie soon. Very soon.

CHAPTER NINETEEN

Enda Barn, Kart Barn

When Minn woke, she found Runa sleeping on the ground.

"Wake up, wake up, Runa, it's time to go! I'm almost home, I'm almost home!"

Runa lifted her head but her expression told Minn that something was not right. Her eyes lacked the gleam that Minn was so used to seeing, and her wings felt heavy and clumsy. She lay on the ground, weak and sick and unable to move. Runa looked like she was dying.

Minn wanted to get home more than anything in the world. Even so, there was only one thing she could do. She had to save Runa.

Minn raced toward the road where she spotted a pair of men having coffee and eating crackers at a nearby picnic table. They had a dog with them, so Minn boldly went right up to the dog and chattered in his face. She gained his attention by chirping and snapping, then nipping his nose. She bit the dog just hard enough to make him chase her, hoping his owners would follow him.

The dog was Balder. He started chasing Minn this way and that, and Minn ran as fast as she could to keep from getting caught. When Minn made it to Runa, she dove into a thicket of weeds and waited. The dog came upon the swan and began to sniff and then bellow. Just as Minn hoped, the men followed Balder into the weeds.

"Hey, what do we have here?" asked the taller of the two as they approached Runa.

"I think this swan is sick," said the other man. "She looks tired and weak. She's not injured, so I wonder if she ate something she shouldn't have. Swans dig deep for grit when they eat, and sometimes they swallow leftover lead shot or lead fishing sinkers. We better help her."

Minn watched as one of the men scooped Runa up in his arms and carried her to the front seat of his truck. He put a blanket

over her, while the other man sat next to
her, keeping her quiet. The dog went into
the back of the truck and sat quietly. They
would take her to an animal hospital and
get her the help she needed. Minn was
happy to see Runa go and hadn't given a
single thought to the fact that now she was
in Duluth with no way of getting home.

CHAPTER TWENTY
Otso

As Minn watched the truck pull away she said goodbye to Runa. But Runa was too sick to respond. So she hollered as loud as she could, "I'll be okay, Runa, don't you worry. I'll make it home. I know I will!"

And then Minn heard a very deep voice come from behind.

"Where's home?"

It was Otso, a mature American black bear who had been wandering through the north woods. He often went from Duluth to more northern parts, and then back again. He ate well in the north woods, northern pike and walleye from the small fresh lakes, honey and grubs and all sorts of berries.

"Where's home?" asked Otso again. Minn wasn't sure if the bear was friendly, and so decided to scramble deep into the woods

and far away from him. She tried to get fast footing, but instead skittered across a patch of pine needles. It was then that she heard the deep bawling sound. "I'm so lonely, I'm so lonely," cried the black bear. Minn stopped. She stood tall and looked the bear straight in the eyes. She knew how he felt. Minn crept up to Otso and they spoke together, exchanging stories about adventure and loneliness, about the north and family, about being lost and looking for home.

As Minn told about Gerdie, Otso listened carefully. Something in Minn's words rang through his heart and his mind, as black bears are very good at remembering things that happened long ago.

"I know Gerdie," said Otso thoughtfully. "Four years ago, when I was a young cub, I had no mother or father, no brother or sisters. Gerdie found me out in the woods and took me home. She fed me wild blueberries and oatmeal pancakes, fresh meat and corn. She taught me how to be a bear in the wild."

Minn liked knowing that Otso knew about Gerdie. It made her feel like they had a common bond and would be friends no matter what. Otso felt the same way.

At that, the bear stood on all fours and shook his coat back and forth and announced to Minn, "I know how to get you home. I promise." When he finished speaking, Otso lowered his head and told Minn to climb up.

And finally, Minn met someone who was able to get her home to Gerdie. It wasn't a swan or an eagle, but a lumbering black bear that was simply returning a favor to someone who had been kind to him a long time ago.

CHAPTER TWENTY-ONE

Heading Home

The pair began to head toward Lake Superior, as Otso thought it might be a good idea to get something to eat along the shores. He liked to eat often, he said, and take naps in the middle of the day.

The day was full of sunshine and the scent of new grasses, and Otso enjoyed padding along the dark rocks near the shore. Every so often, he would dash across the highway that followed the shore and head into the woods, hiding from cars or people. He told Minn how it seemed as if people were afraid of him, and he didn't really understand why. He said that he had a kind heart full of friendship, and it made him feel sad when people hollered or ran away when they saw him. Minn felt sad for Otso when he told her this, because she couldn't imagine why people wouldn't take a chance to get to know a fellow first.

The pair continued north, where there were plenty of budding trees and bushes from which to eat. Whenever it was time to nap, Otso would find a cool shady place to lay himself down, and Minn would go into the woods to find nuts and berries of her own choosing.

They traveled for days this way, each getting to know the other a little better. One day, as Otso was napping in the woods at the outskirts of Silver Bay, Minn went off to find lunch. She spotted a pile of pinecones that must have fallen during a strong wind, and thought perhaps there would be some good seeds inside. She first dug her nose in, then her whole body. She was deep into the pile and foraging when all of a sudden SWOOP! a cooper's hawk grabbed her and darted away.

"Otso, Otso," she cried. Her high-pitched screeches woke Otso, who spotted the hawk making its way through the woods. Right away Otso began to follow the hawk.

As the hawk made its way through the forest and into town, Otso gave no thought to his own safety as he followed it. Otso was fast, and Minn kept chirping and squealing so that Otso would know right where they were. The hawk flew right up a street where there were houses to the left and the right, with Otso following behind. They went up a hill and through rows of gardens and streets.

Otso barely paid attention to the people that were scrambling from their yards into their homes. Cars slowed, doors slammed, and Otso had one thing on his mind—to save Minn.

As the hawk changed course and headed down an alley, it began to lose its grip on Minn.

Minn went sliding through its talons and into the air—straight into a large rusty barrel of garbage. The hawk circled with the intent of grabbing Minn again, but Otso charged and began to bat him away with his large black paws. The hawk dipped and darted at Otso, who paid no attention to him. Otso heard Minn in the garbage can and so began to dig fast and furiously through the rubbish to find Minn. Leftover food and papers went flying this way and that, and as the people in their homes watched through their windows, they could think only one thing. It was a mad bear in town.

All of a sudden three cars surrounded Otso, and Otso was scared.

A man stepped out of his car and Otso looked him straight in the eyes. The man had a long pole with a loop on it, and Otso had to do something. Minn chirped at Otso to get in the barrel, which was now lying empty on its side.

Otso did and Minn scrambled in after him.
Right then, the weight of the huge bear
made the barrel roll. And roll.
It rolled fast down the hill and past the
cars, with Minn and Otso inside. It bumped
and rolled all the way to the edge of the
forest they had come out of and came to a

quick stop when it hit a group of birch trees. Otso and Minn were tossed out of the barrel and went running into the woods, finally finding a place to stop and rest by a cool stream.

And although Otso and Minn recovered from their mishap, most people who saw the scene never forgot about the day a mad bear came crashing through town.

CHAPTER TWENTY-TWO
The Cabin Door

Minn and Otso journeyed northwest for days, traveling through deep dense woods and by cool, freshwater lakes. This time, Otso never let Minn out of his sight.

131

Minn knew they were getting closer, as the song of loons at night and the smell of wood smoke in the air told her the cabin was not far. By now, Otso was just as eager to see Gerdie as Minn was, for renewing an old friendship seemed like a refreshing thing for an old bear to do.

When they were within sight of the cabin, Minn climbed off Otso's back and raced up the trail to the front door.

But the door was closed.

Minn found a little hole in a window screen and burst through it and called out for Gerdie. "Gerdie," she cried, "I'm home, I'm home, I'm really home!"

But no one answered.

The cabin was quiet. There were no fresh flowers in Gerdie's blue vase, no warm

treats baking in the oven. The curtains were closed, and the quilt was neat and tidy on the bed, as if it hadn't been slept in for a very long time.

Minn called out again, but still nobody answered. Gerdie wasn't there.

Minn looked around. Home wasn't home without Gerdie. Minn began to weep. She tucked herself into a little ball and wept near the woodstove, hoping that, at any moment, Gerdie would come home.

Minn stayed there for what seemed to be a very long time, not wanting to open her eyes to see again how different the cabin looked without Gerdie. And then she heard a noise. First it was a small rustle, then a scraping sound. Minn heard the stepping sounds of feet across the pine floors and looked up, hoping to see Gerdie.

But it was Paavo, Minn's fox friend.

Paavo came in through a small hole in one of the logs and greeted Minn warmly. Sulo the raccoon followed behind, and then came Aapo the pine marten and Floris the skunk. They were all there, nuzzling and greeting Minn, letting her know how happy they were that she was finally home.

Minn was happy to see them, too, and let them know this in the silly way a white-footed mouse will do. But quickly, she changed the subject to ask, "Where's Gerdie?"

Paavo, Floris, Sulo, and Aapo turned serious. Minn could tell by their expressions that something was just not right.

Paavo spoke. "Gerdie is gone. She's been gone for a very long time."

Minn didn't understand. "Where could she be?" she cried. "Where did Gerdie go?"

Paavo lowered her head and softly said, "She's out looking for you. She thinks you ran away."

Minn sobbed. She had worked so hard to make it home, and now Gerdie wasn't there. It just wasn't right. Minn wanted to go in her drawer to think about

To All Willing
Heart of Wisconsin
Please Do Come!
Cheese Jamboree
One First Prize Cheese
Good Treats and Games
Contest
Cheese Smorgasbord Try
Any Thing You Like!

all the places Gerdie might be searching. Would she look for me in town? Would she look for me by the lake?

As Minn crawled across the dresser top to make her way inside, something caught her eye. It was a poster for a cheese-eating contest. It said:

To All Willing:
Heart of Wisconsin Cheese Jamboree
Please Do Come!
One First Prize Cheese Contest
Good Treats and Games
Cheese Smorgasbord, Try Any Thing
You Like!

That's it! Gerdie must think I ran away to a cheese-eating contest, and she is looking for me there! Minn raced through the cabin, gathering any spare crumbs or seeds she could find, storing them in her cheeks for later. It was going to be a long journey, she thought to herself, but she had to find Gerdie and bring her home.

When Minn finished preparing, she went outside onto the porch. Paavo, Floris, Aapo, and Sulo were still there, getting to know Otso a little bit better. Minn puffed out her chest and drew a deep breath of courage before telling the others she was on her way to find Gerdie. But before Minn even had the chance to speak, Otso and the others announced that they would go with her and help in any way they could.

Minn looked at her friends with fondness. It was a kind and generous offer, but Minn knew this was something she had to do— alone. *Enda barn, kart barn.* Only child, dear child ... She was on her way.

And so that is how it came to be that Minn, a white-footed mouse from Minnesota, went scurrying into Wisconsin on an early summer day. Gerdie had been the only real mother she had ever known, and now because Gerdie was out looking for Minn, Minn had to take a big chance on how to find her, and bring her back home.

COMING SOON...

Mitt & Minn at the Wisconsin Cheese Jamboree

Mitten Press is proud of its series of chapter books about the adventures of a pair of white-footed mice named Mitt and Minn. In this story, we introduce Minn who arrives in northern Minnesota in a bushel of cherries. In Book One, we met Mitt in his home state of Michigan. Book Three will see the two mice head to the Cheese Jamboree in Wisconsin—Mitt in search of his mitten home and Minn looking for her friend, Gerdie. You'll be amazed by what they learn there and where their adventures will take them next!

Join Mitt and Minn's Midwest Readers by sending your email address to the publisher at ljohnson@mittenpress.com. You will receive updates as new books in the series are completed and fun activities to challenge what you know about the Midwest states.

Book One: Mitt, the Michigan Mouse ISBN: 1-58726-303-3
Book Two: Minn from Minnesota ISBN: 1-58726-304-1
Book Three: Mitt & Minn at the Wisconsin Cheese Jamboree
   ISBN: 1-58726-305-X (March 2007)

www.mittenpress.com

CANADA
CA
NORTH DAKOTA
AGASSIZ NATIONAL WILDLIFE REFUGE
UPPER RED LAKE
LOWER RED LAKE
RED LAKE RIVER
ITASKA STATE PARK
GRAND RAPIDS
MINNESOTA
ALEXANDRIA
MINNEAPOLIS
ST. PAUL
IOW